This Little Tiger book belongs to:

_____

_____

_____

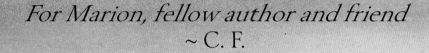

For Marion, fellow author and friend
~ C. F.

For my nephew, Jamie Wernert
~ T. M.

LITTLE TIGER PRESS
An imprint of Magi Publications
1 The Coda Centre, 189 Munster Road, London SW6 6AW
www.littletigerpress.com

First published in Great Britain 2005
This edition published 2008

Text copyright © Claire Freedman 2004 • Illustrations copyright © Tina Macnaughton 2004
Claire Freedman and Tina Macnaughton have asserted their rights
to be identified as the author and illustrator of this work
under the Copyright, Designs and Patents Act, 1988

A CIP catalogue record for this book is available from the British Library

Printed in China

10 9 8 7 6 5 4 3 2 1

Snuggle Up, Sleepy Ones

Claire Freedman   Tina Macnaughton

LITTLE TIGER PRESS

London

The sun paints the sky
a warm, glowing red.
It's time to stop playing,
it's time for bed.

In the soft swampy mud
baby hippo, so snug,
Cuddles up close
for a big hippo hug.

Through wild, waving grasses
shy antelope roam.

It's been a long day,
they're ready for home.

Bold leopard cubs rest
from practising roars.
They snuggle together,
all tired, tangled paws.

Whilst up in the treetops
birds twitter and cheep,

Till quieter and quieter,
they fall fast asleep.

Below in their nests
baby porcupines all
Curl up, so snug tight,
in one spiky ball.

With tired, drooping necks
giraffe flop to the ground.
Sheltered and watched over.
Safe and sound.

And mischievous monkeys
shout down from the trees,
"It's not really dark yet.
Five more minutes, please!"

Zebras lay panting,
tired out from their play.
They sink into sleep
as the sun slips away.

Moths come a-fluttering,
bats flitter by.
Elephants rumble
their deep lullaby.

Shadows grow deeper,
the lion cubs doze.
Drowsy heads nod,
little eyes start to close.

Stars twinkle brightly,
the moon softly gleams.
Snuggle up, sleepy ones.
Hush now, sweet dreams!

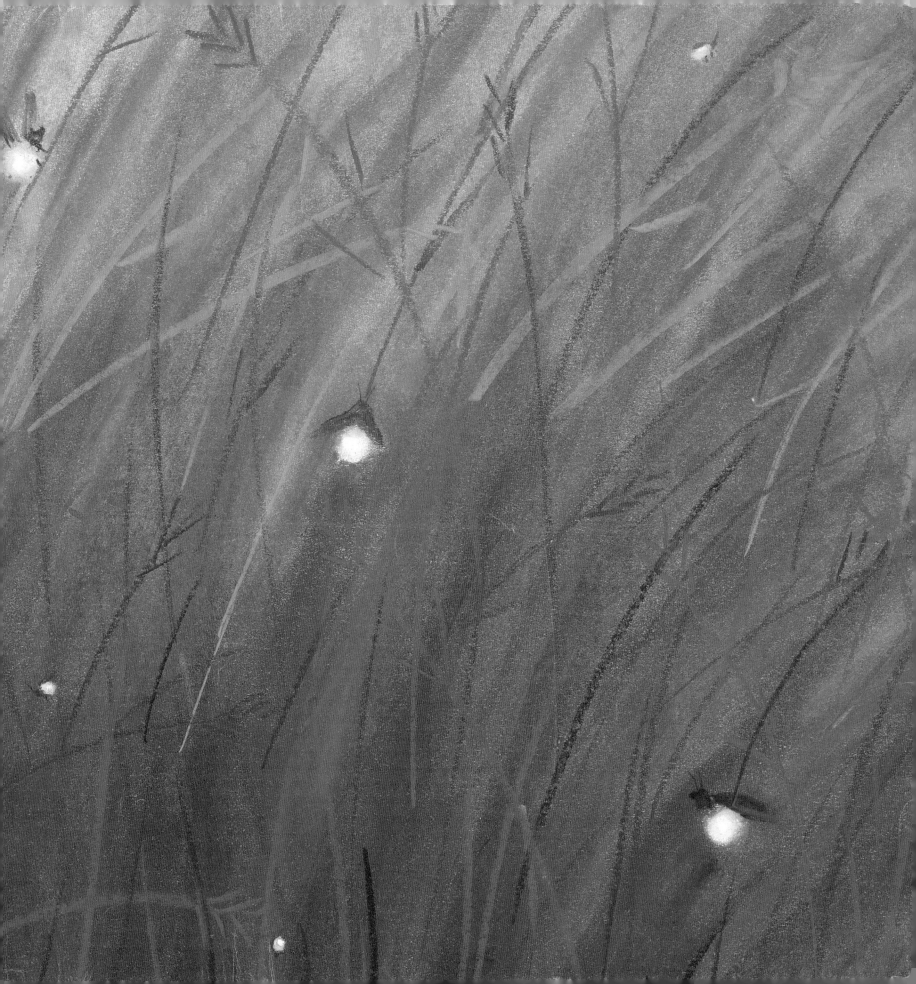

Snuggle up with a lullaby ...

Daylight dims, the sky turns red,
Time to stop playing, time for bed.
Hush, little baby, the stars are bright.
Snuggle up, sleepy one, kiss goodnight!

Baby hippo cuddles mum,
Warm and snug as the day is done.
Hush, little baby, the stars are bright.
Snuggle up, sleepy one, kiss goodnight!

Birds in the treetops twitter and cheep,
Now they are quiet as they fall asleep.
Tired from play the lion cubs doze,
Their eyes are already tightly closed.
Hush, little baby, the stars are bright.
Snuggle up, sleepy one, kiss goodnight!

All the animals are in bed,
It's time to rest your heavy head.
Hush, little baby, the stars are bright.
Snuggle up, sleepy one, kiss goodnight!

Other recent titles in this series

For information regarding any other Little Tiger Tales Picture Book and
CD Sets, or for our catalogue, please contact us: Little Tiger Press,
1 The Coda Centre, 189 Munster Road, London SW6 6AW, UK
Tel: 020 7385 6333 Fax: 020 7385 7333
e-mail: info@littletiger.co.uk
www.littletigerpress.com